KIDS' SPORTS STORIES

HOCKEY HERO

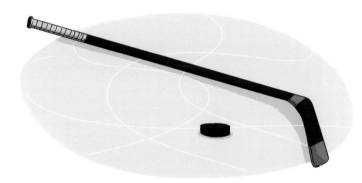

by Elliott Smith

illustrated by Diego Funck

PICTURE WINDOW BOOKS
a capstone imprint

Kids' Sports Stories is published by Picture Window Books, an imprint of Capstone.
1710 Roe Crest Drive, North Mankato, Minnesota 56003
www.capstonepub.com

**Library of Congress Cataloging-in-Publication Data is available
on the Library of Congress website.**
ISBN 978-1-5158-7098-2 (library binding)
ISBN 978-1-5158-7286-3 (paperback)
ISBN 978-1-5158-7132-3 (eBook PDF)

Summary: Grace loves the sport of hockey. Out on the ice, no one can touch her speed. But she can't shoot, and her frustration tempts her to quit the team. With help from her teammate Myles, Grace strengthens her skills. Then she leans on his encouragement when an injury takes him out of a playoff game and requires Grace to be the team hero.

Designer: Ted Williams

Printed in the United States of America.
PA117

TABLE OF CONTENTS

Glossary

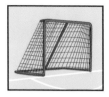 **goal**—the area within which players must put the puck to score

 **goalie**—the player who guards the net and tries to keep the other team from scoring

 **hat trick**—when a hockey player scores three goals in a single game

 **puck**—a rubber disk that teams try to shoot in the goal

 **rink**—an enclosed area of ice used for skating or hockey

Chapter 1
HIT THE ICE

Grace and her friend Myles sat by the ice rink. They put on their skates. They tightened the laces.

"Ready for practice?" Grace asked.

"I'm always ready to hit the ice!" Myles said.

The two friends grabbed their hockey sticks. They joined their team on the ice. Coach blew his whistle.

"OK, Polar Bears!" Coach said. "We have a big game coming up. You have practiced hard the past couple weeks. But we need more work on basic skills. Let's start today with skating drills."

Grace loved skating drills. She watched Coach set up cones on the ice. When it was her turn, she went smoothly around each one.

"No problem!" Grace said.

Next, the team lined up to race. When the whistle blew, everyone took off.

WHOOSH! They skated to the other end of the rink and back. Grace easily beat her teammates.

Shooting drills were next. Grace was a terrific skater, but she wasn't very good with a puck. She watched as Myles shot the puck into the goal on his first try. He always scored the most goals for the team.

Grace tried next. Her shot flew far past the net.

"Try again, Grace," Coach said. "Take your time."

Grace gripped the stick. She took another shot. Again, the puck flew past the net. She tried three more times. Each time, she missed the net.

Chapter 2
SLOW IT DOWN

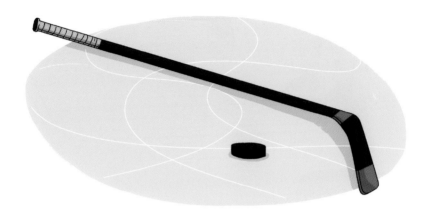

Coach blew his whistle. Practice ended. Grace skated sadly to the bench. Myles sat next to her.

"I should quit," Grace said. "The big game is coming up. I can't shoot. I don't want our team to lose because of me."

Myles shook his head. "No way, Grace. We all need you! You're our best skater," he said.

"But I can't shoot!" Grace said.

Myles thought for a second. "Let's ask our parents if we can stay after practice next time," he said. "We'll work together. You can help me skate faster. And I can help you shoot better. OK?"

"OK," Grace said.

Every day after practice, Grace and Myles worked on their skills. Grace helped Myles get more speed. He learned how to push harder off the ice with his skates.

Myles tried to get Grace to slow down.
She always skated as fast as she could to
the goal. When it was time to shoot, she
missed. She couldn't control the puck.

"You're going too fast," Myles said. "Slow down and keep your eye on the net."

Grace tried again. She did what Myles told her. And for the first time, her shot went in.

"I did it!" she cried.

"Yes! Now do it again, just like that," Myles said.

Grace lifted her stick and . . . *WHIFF!*
She missed the puck.

"Your eyes were closed, Grace!" Myles
said. "Don't close your eyes!"

Grace laughed. Myles passed her the puck
again. This time, she kept her eyes open.

Grace shot the puck. It didn't go in, but she felt better about shooting. By the end of the week, she didn't want to quit the team anymore. She wanted to play.

Chapter 3
A SURPRISE STAR

The day of the big game came. Grace and the other Polar Bears couldn't sit still. The other team, the Dragons, was the best. Coach gathered everyone together.

"Remember to have fun," he said with a smile. "Go, Polar Bears!"

The first group of players went out on the ice. Myles was one of them. Grace watched from the bench.

The Dragons scored a quick goal. Then Myles took the puck. He zoomed toward the net. Before he could shoot, he slipped and fell. He was hurt! His ankle was twisted. Coach helped him off the ice.

"Grace, you're in!" Coach said.

Grace gulped. She tried to remember what Myles had taught her. All she could do was try her best.

Grace felt good on the ice. A couple
minutes in, Hallie passed her the puck.
Grace slowed down. She kept her eyes on
the net and took a shot. The puck went
between the goalie's legs. Score!

Soon the Dragons took the lead again. But Grace was playing to win. She grabbed the puck. She used her speed to get ahead of everyone else. The goalie tried to block her. Grace skated around him and tapped the puck into the net. Score!

Both teams played hard. With one minute left, the game was tied. *Tick, tick, tick* went the clock. Logan passed the puck to Grace. She was ready! She brought her stick back and . . . *WHAP*! Her shot went over the goalie's shoulder and into the net!

The buzzer sounded. The Polar Bears won the game, 3–2.

Myles cheered the loudest. "Grace, you scored a hat trick!" he said. "You're a hero!"

"Thanks for your help, Myles!" Grace said. "I'm really glad I didn't give up!"

29

HOCKEY JERSEY FUN

The Polar Bears need a new logo for their jerseys. Create a few designs for Grace and her team to choose from!

What You Need:
- a piece of construction paper, any color
- a large soup can
- crayons or markers
- scissors
- old magazines
- glue
- add-ons, such as glitter, ribbon, or pom-poms (optional)

What You Do:
1. Trace as many soup cans on the paper as will fit.
2. Cut out the circles.
3. Make a different logo on each circle. Be sure to include the team name. You can write it by hand or use letters cut from the magazines and glue them in place.
4. Add a drawing of a polar bear, a snowflake, hockey sticks, or other objects to your logos.
5. Show your logos to your friends and family. Have them vote for their favorite!

REPLAY IT

Take another look at this illustration. How do you think Grace is feeling during this moment of the big game? Pretend you are Grace and write a letter to your grandparents about it.

ABOUT THE AUTHOR

Elliott Smith is a former sports reporter who covered athletes in all sports from high school to the pros. He is one of the authors of the Natural Thrills series about extreme outdoor sports. In his spare time, he likes playing sports with his two children, going to the movies, and adding to his collection of Pittsburgh Steelers memorabilia.

ABOUT
THE ILLUSTRATOR

Diego Funck designs and illustrates children's books and other publications, often working with a Belgian illustration team called Coco Zool. Since 2005, his work has appeared in gallery shows in Belgium, France, and England. When he's not drawing or painting, Diego loves to watch movie trailers and dig in his vegetable garden. He currently lives in Brussels, Belgium.